GRANDPA'S HAL-LA-LOO-YA HAMBONE!

BY JOE HAYES
ILLUSTRATED BY ANTONIO CASTRO L.

CINCO PUNTOS PRESS
www.cincopuntos.com

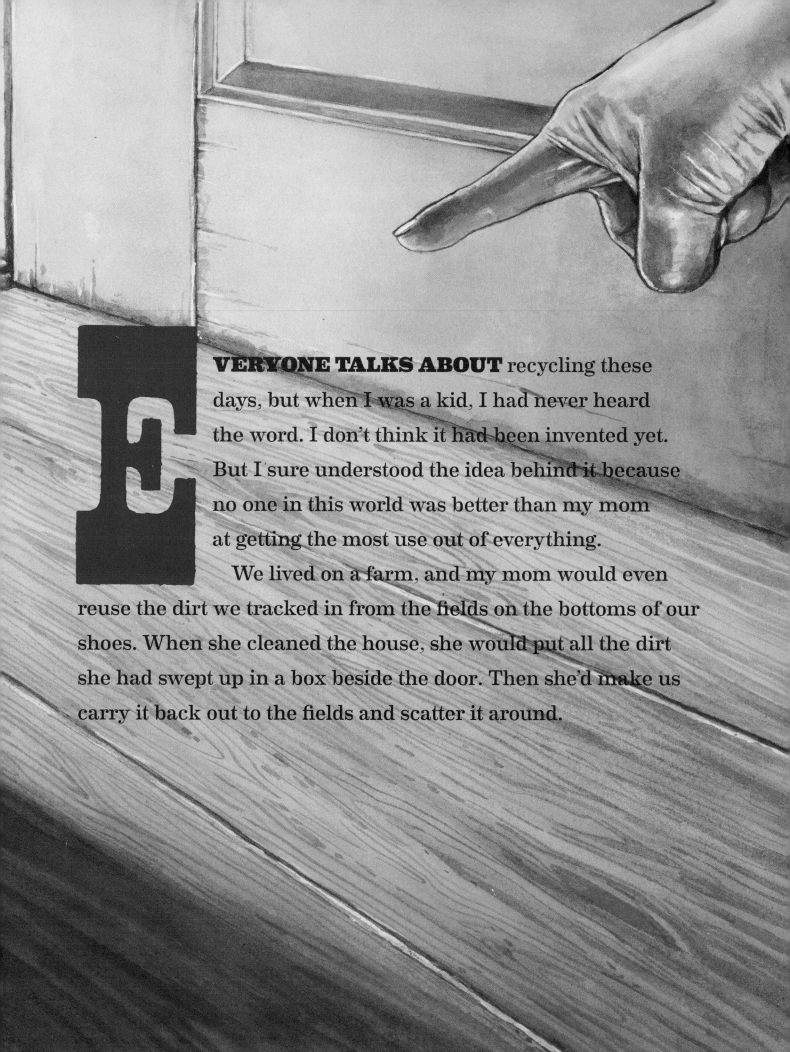

EVERYONE TALKS ABOUT recycling these days, but when I was a kid, I had never heard the word. I don't think it had been invented yet. But I sure understood the idea behind it because no one in this world was better than my mom at getting the most use out of everything.

We lived on a farm, and my mom would even reuse the dirt we tracked in from the fields on the bottoms of our shoes. When she cleaned the house, she would put all the dirt she had swept up in a box beside the door. Then she'd make us carry it back out to the fields and scatter it around.

MY MOM WOULD SAY, "As poor as the soil is around here, we can't afford to have you kids tracking all the fertilizer from the fields into the house on the bottoms of your shoes." Of course, if you think about it you'll see that when we carried the dirt back out to the fields, we got more dirt on the bottoms of our shoes.

My mom wasn't right about everything. But she sure was right that the soil was bad around our end of the county. Hardly anything would grow in that dirt. Except beans. For some reason, beans always did fine.

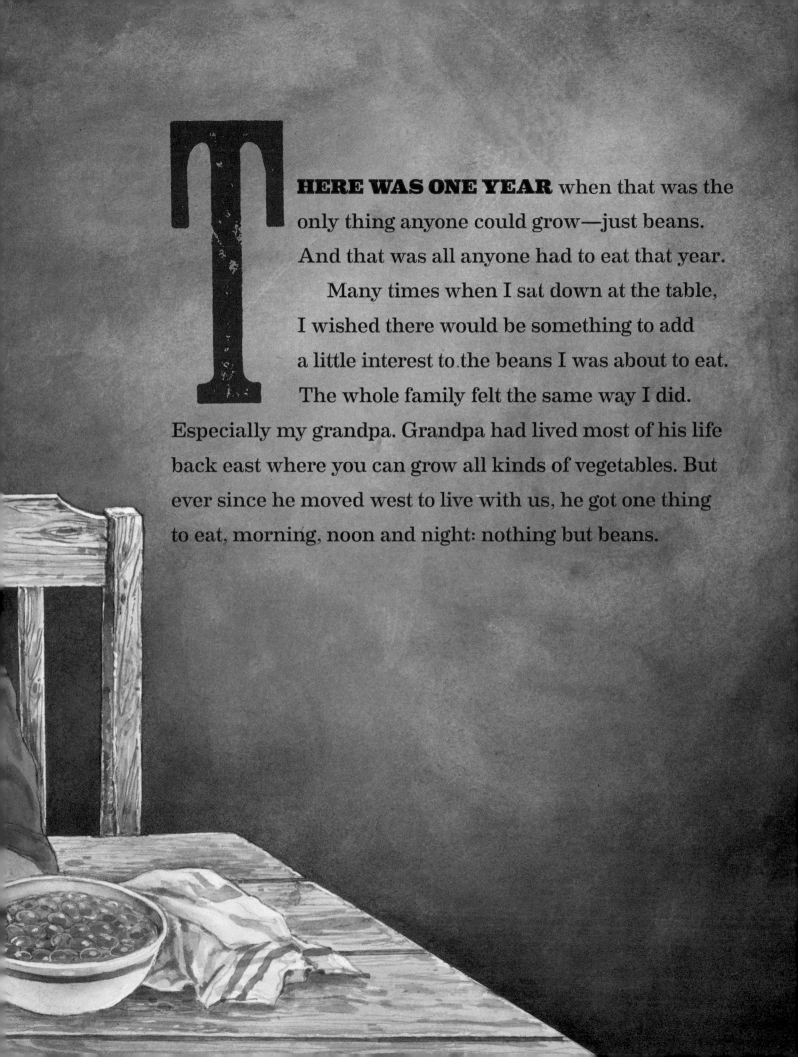

THERE WAS ONE YEAR when that was the only thing anyone could grow—just beans. And that was all anyone had to eat that year. Many times when I sat down at the table, I wished there would be something to add a little interest to the beans I was about to eat. The whole family felt the same way I did. Especially my grandpa. Grandpa had lived most of his life back east where you can grow all kinds of vegetables. But ever since he moved west to live with us, he got one thing to eat, morning, noon and night: nothing but beans.

AND THEN MY DAD decided to take a big risk. He filled several sacks with beans and loaded them onto his pickup. He drove and drove until he came to a place where beans weren't so plentiful, and he was able to sell his load and head back home.

BUT WITH ALL THE COST of traveling out and traveling back home again, he didn't make much money from the venture. When he went to the store to spend his earnings, all he could afford to buy was a big hambone. He brought the hambone home and when Sunday came around my mom used it to flavor our beans for Sunday dinner. I'll never forget that dinner as long as I live.

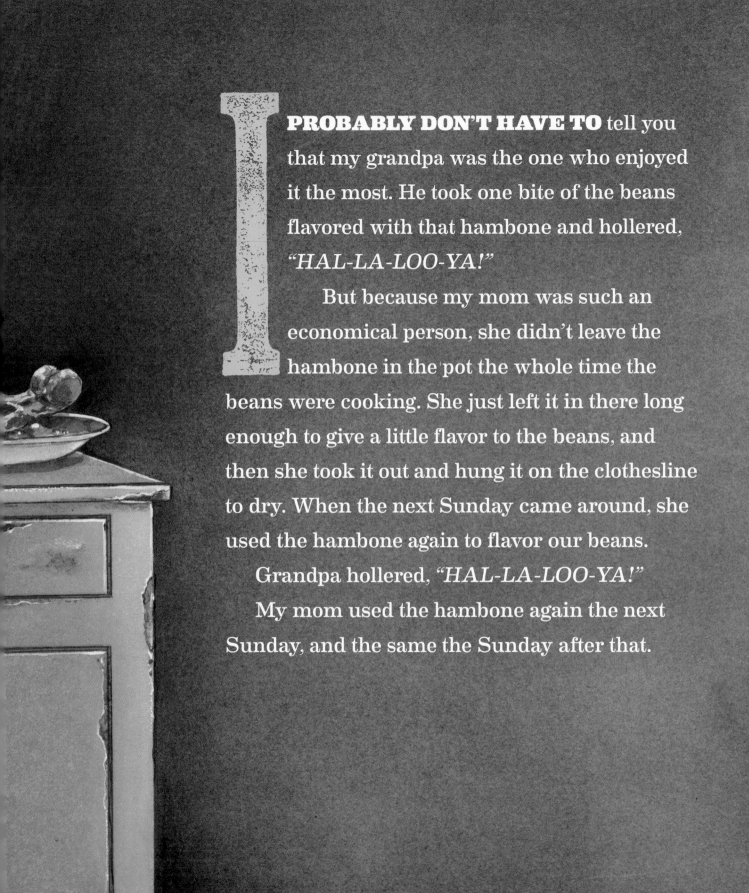

I PROBABLY DON'T HAVE TO tell you that my grandpa was the one who enjoyed it the most. He took one bite of the beans flavored with that hambone and hollered, *"HAL-LA-LOO-YA!"*

But because my mom was such an economical person, she didn't leave the hambone in the pot the whole time the beans were cooking. She just left it in there long enough to give a little flavor to the beans, and then she took it out and hung it on the clothesline to dry. When the next Sunday came around, she used the hambone again to flavor our beans.

Grandpa hollered, *"HAL-LA-LOO-YA!"*

My mom used the hambone again the next Sunday, and the same the Sunday after that.

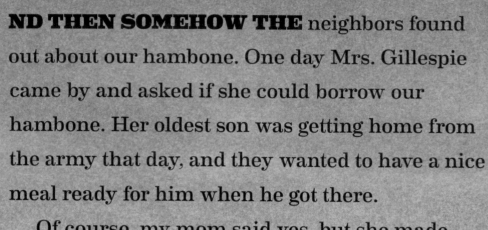**ND THEN SOMEHOW THE** neighbors found out about our hambone. One day Mrs. Gillespie came by and asked if she could borrow our hambone. Her oldest son was getting home from the army that day, and they wanted to have a nice meal ready for him when he got there.

Of course, my mom said yes, but she made Mrs. Gillespie promise she'd only leave it in the pot for a little while and then dry it out really well.

IT WASN'T LONG BEFORE our hambone would be gone two or three days out of every week! Every time some family was celebrating a special occasion—a birthday, a baptism, a wedding anniversary—they'd come by and borrow our hambone.

My grandpa would always manage to wrangle an invitation to dinner with whatever family was serving some flavored beans.

And then one Saturday, Mrs. McIvey came by. Her daughter was going to get married, and she asked if she could borrow the hambone to make a nice wedding supper. My mom said she could.

OF COURSE, MRS. McIVEY knew she should invite Grandpa to the wedding, so she did. *"HAL-LA-LOO-YA!"* Grandpa hollered and he hurried out back to the well to wash his face.

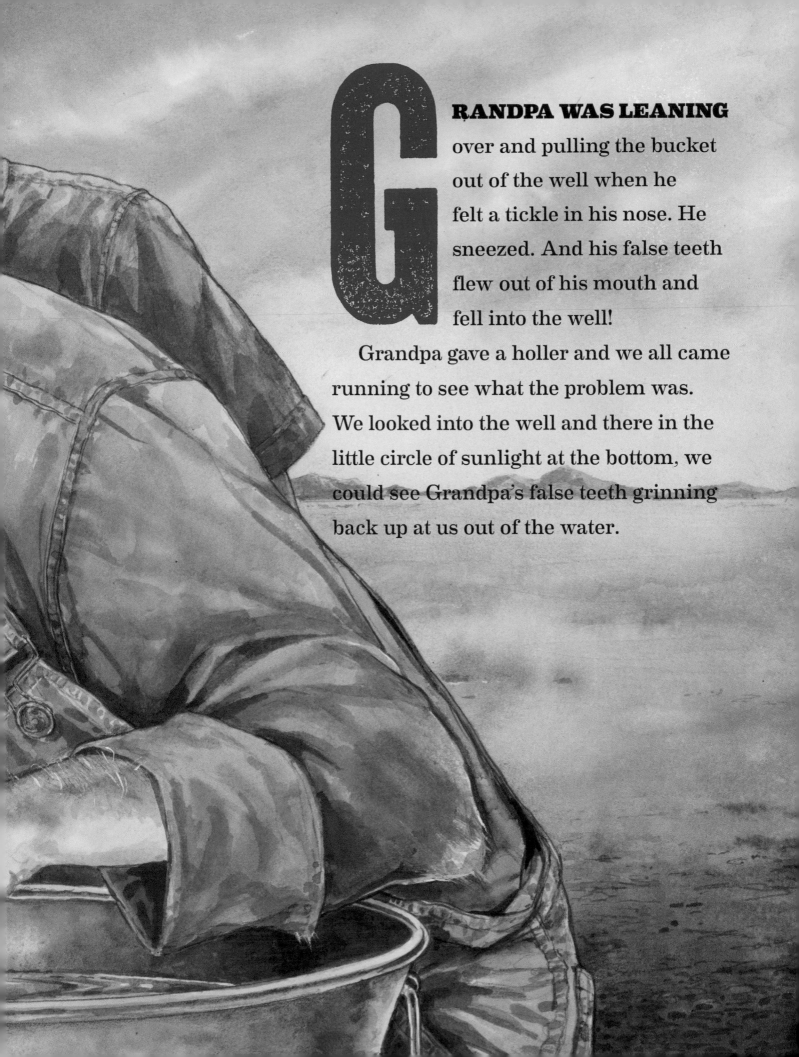

G

GRANDPA WAS LEANING over and pulling the bucket out of the well when he felt a tickle in his nose. He sneezed. And his false teeth flew out of his mouth and fell into the well!

Grandpa gave a holler and we all came running to see what the problem was. We looked into the well and there in the little circle of sunlight at the bottom, we could see Grandpa's false teeth grinning back up at us out of the water.

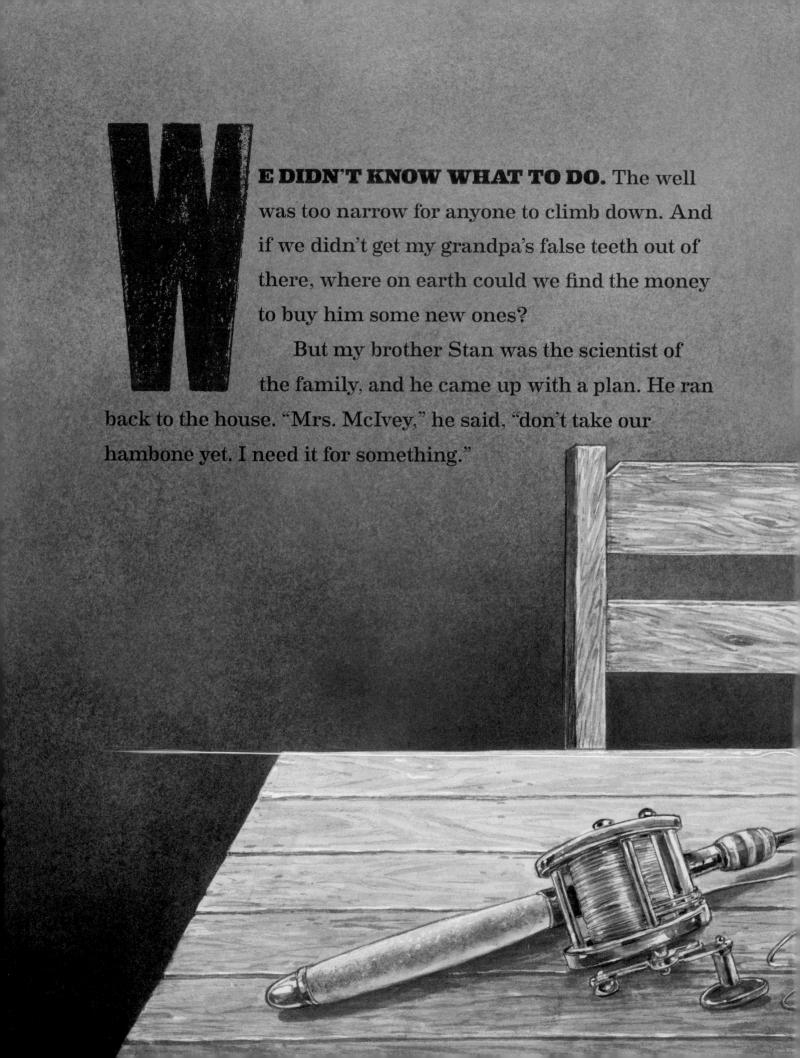

WE DIDN'T KNOW WHAT TO DO. The well was too narrow for anyone to climb down. And if we didn't get my grandpa's false teeth out of there, where on earth could we find the money to buy him some new ones?

But my brother Stan was the scientist of the family, and he came up with a plan. He ran back to the house. "Mrs. McIvey," he said, "don't take our hambone yet. I need it for something."

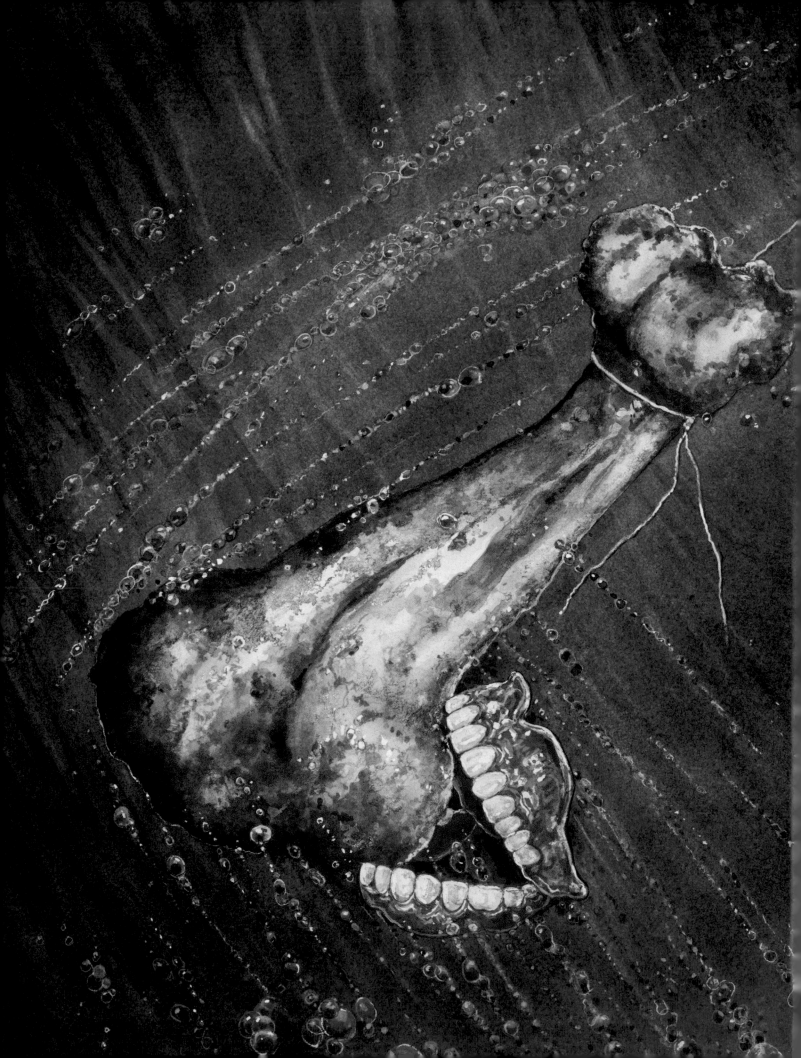

MY BROTHER TIED THE hambone onto the end of a fishing line. He lowered it into the well and sort of dangled it in front of Grandpa's false teeth. Well, Grandpa's false teeth had grown so used to eating beans flavored with that hambone that they opened right up and clamped onto it.

My brother reeled in the fishing line and up came Grandpa's false teeth, fastened tight to the hambone.

EVERYONE IN THE family hollered, "*HAL-LA-LOO-YA!*" But the false teeth were fastened so tight that we had a terrible time trying to pry them loose. In the tug-of-war we were having with the false teeth, the fishing line snapped. That sudden jerk startled the false teeth. They loosened their grip on the hambone. And the hambone fell into the well!

I **WANTED TO TIE MY** Grandpa's false teeth onto the fishing line and lower them down to get the hambone out of there, but my dad said we'd better not. If the fishing line should happen to break, he explained, Grandpa's false teeth would end up clamped onto the hambone at the bottom of the well forever.

Mrs. McIvey was terribly disappointed. Well, half the county was disappointed, for that matter. It was like the end of an era.

BUT DO YOU KNOW THAT up until the time I grew up and left home, folks would still come by to get water from our well to cook their beans in? They always said that beans cooked in that water had a special taste to them. They wouldn't come right out and say they tasted like ham. That might be stretching things a bit and folks around there didn't ever exaggerate the truth. But they would have a special flavor. There's no denying that.

Yes, sir! Neighbors would take one taste of beans cooked in that water and holler, *"HAL-LA-LOO-YA!"*

Printed in the U.S.

First Edition
10 9 8 7 6 5 4 3 2 1

Library of Congress Cataloging-in-Publication Data

Names: Hayes, Joe, author. | Castro, Antonio, 1941- illustrator.
Title: Grandpa's ha-la-loo-ya hambone! / by Joe Hayes ; illustrated by Antonio Castro L.
Description: First edition. | El Paso, TX : Cinco Puntos Press, [2016] |
Summary: When Grandpa's false teeth fall down a well, a recycled hambone which has flavored the bean dinners of many families in his poor farm community, is used to retrieve his dentures.
Identifiers: LCCN 2016014778 | ISBN 978-1-941026-55-7 (paperback) | ISBN 978-1-941026-54-0 (cloth) | ISBN 978-1-941026-56-5 (e-book)
Subjects: | CYAC: Grandfathers—Fiction. | Farm life—Fiction. | Southwest, New—Fiction. | Tall tales. | Humorous stories.
| BISAC: JUVENILE FICTION / Humorous Stories. | JUVENILE FICTION / Boys & Men. | JUVENILE FICTION /Action & Adventure / General. | JUVENILE FICTION / Imagination & Play.
Classification: LCC PZ7.H31474 Gr 2016 | DDC [E]—dc23
LC record available at https://lccn.loc.gov/2016014778

Book and cover design by Antonio Castro H.